The Coffee Can Kid

Written by Jan M. Czech

Illustrated by Maurie J. Manning

Child & Family Press   Washington, DC

The chair teetered under Annie's feet. She rooted through the tangle of winter hats and mittens on the top shelf of the hall closet.

"There it is." Annie leaned farther into the closet. Something blue peeked at her from behind a shoebox. She reached for it. Her finger-tips brushed cool metal.

Annie stretched. The chair tipped. She grabbed the object as the chair scooted out from under her.

CRASH!

Down she went in a heap
with the family's mittens,
scarves, hats, and gloves.

"Are you okay?" Her father hurried from the kitchen. Annie shrugged and held up the blue coffee can clutched in her hands.

"Tell me the story about the coffee can kid." She smiled up at her father. He grinned back and flopped down onto the nest of hats, gloves, mittens, and scarves.

"You don't want to hear that old story again," he said.

Annie cuddled close and picked at the plastic top of the can.

"It's my favorite. Please?" Annie ran her fingers up and down the cool metal and counted the ridges. There were six. Just like her age, six years old.

"The coffee can kid was born in a faraway land on the other side of the world," said Annie's father.

Annie drummed on the top of the can with her fingers.

BUM bum bum bum,

BUM, bum bum bum...

"The coffee can kid

was born on a

cold January day."

Annie shivered and hugged the can closer.

"She was born in the hilly country, far from a city."

"In a hospital with doctors and nurses?" Annie asked.

"No, in a small hut. The home of her grandmother. A fire in the woodstove warmed the room, and lanterns lit the baby's way."

"Was she beautiful, like a princess?" Annie twisted a lock of her chin-length hair around her finger.

"The coffee can kid was the most beautiful baby in the world. She was healthy and happy. There was a problem, though," said Annie's father.

"What? Did she cry too much? Did she eat too much?"

"The coffee can kid couldn't stay in her grandmother's hut," he said.

Annie shook the can. Something inside rustled like dry leaves in a fall breeze.

"Her mother couldn't take care of her. She was too young and the grandmother was too old. There was no money and no husband. The baby's mother had to make a plan," said Annie's father.

"Wait, Daddy, you left out a part." Her father looked down at Annie. He grinned.

"What part did I forget?"

"The part where the coffee can kid gets a name," said Annie.

"Oh, yes, the name. Her mother thought and thought. She wanted to give her baby a very special name because she loved her so much."

"What did she name the baby?"

"Dong Hee. The baby's name was Dong Hee."

"That's a funny name," Annie laughed.

"It sounds funny to you because it's in another language."

"What does it mean?" Annie wriggled closer to her father.

"It means Shining Hope. The mother named her baby Shining Hope," said Annie's father.

"I like that. It's prettier than plain old Annie."

She balanced the coffee can

on her fingertips.

Her father lifted his right eyebrow.

"I kind of like plain old Annie." He tickled her and she giggled. The can fell to the floor. Annie grabbed it before it rolled under a nearby rocking chair.

"Dong Hee's mother had a hard decision to make. She loved her baby but knew she didn't have enough money to feed her or buy her clothes. The winter wind whistled down the chimney and rattled the windows. The moon rose in the midnight sky. The hut grew cold. She cuddled Dong Hee. While the baby slept, the mother thought of her choices. By the time the sun rose over the hillside, she had made her plan."

Annie tipped the can forward and back. The contents whispered against its rounded sides.

"The young mother took Dong Hee to the baby home. She told the people there she wanted her Shining Hope to have a good life. The mother filled out many forms and answered many questions. Finally, they said they would do what they could.

"The mother held her baby one last time. She brushed Dong Hee's hair back from her forehead and a tear fell there as she said good-bye."

"Then what happened?" said Annie.

"They found a home for the baby in the United States. Do you know who adopted her?"

"You and Mommy did. The coffee can kid is me."

"Yes. Mommy and I waited and waited for you to come to America. And..."

"Can I open it now?" Annie pried open the plastic top of the can and took out the items inside.

She held up a picture. "This is Dong Hee the day her mother took her to the baby home." The baby was chubby. She scowled at the camera from under wispy, black bangs.

"That's the first picture ever taken of you. What else is inside the can?" her father asked.

"This letter," said Annie. She held up a piece of paper so thin she could see her hand through it. Words covered the page from top to bottom and side to side.

"Read me the letter, Daddy."

"You know I can't read it. The people from the agency told Mommy and me what it said. This is a letter from your birthmother. She wrote it the day she said good-bye."

"What does it say?"

"It says that she loves you, and not a day will go by that she doesn't think of you. It says she hopes you are happy and strong and in a home where there is enough to eat. She hopes you are with people who love you as much as she does."

"I wonder where she is now," Annie said.

"I don't know. I wonder, too."

"Tell me why you keep the picture and the letter in the can, Daddy."

"Your picture is in the can because the lady at the agency said it was the best way to keep it from fading. She found hundreds of families for babies from many countries and she told all of them the same thing. The letter is in the can because we thought it should be with the picture. They are both special."

Annie studied the picture and the letter for a long time. Then she put them back in the blue coffee can. She snapped the lid on tight and ran her fingers up and down the ridges. There were still six.

"Can I look at this whenever I want to?"

"Yes, as long as you're very careful."

Annie looked at the tipped-over chair and the snarl of winter hats and mittens. "I think we should put this on a lower shelf," she said.

She rolled the can between her hands. The things inside fluttered like butterfly wings.